HELLO, MONDARIN DUCK!

WRITTEN BY BAO PHI   ILLUSTRATED BY DION MBD

CAPSTONE EDITIONS
a capstone imprint

Hello, Mandarin Duck! is published by Capstone Editions, an imprint of Capstone.
1710 Roe Crest Drive
North Mankato, Minnesota 56003
www.capstonepub.com

Library of Congress Cataloging-in-Publication Data is available on the Library of Congress website.
ISBN: 978-1-6844-6256-8 (hardcover)
ISBN: 978-1-6844-6338-1 (ebook PDF)

Summary: Twins Hue and Hoa are excited for the May Day parade! While waiting at the park for the parade
to begin, they spot a little duck who seems new to the neighborhood—and looks confused by the crowd and
commotion. How can the twins help the duck get to the pond? Many friends from the neighborhood stop to say
hello and offer suggestions. Teamwork, brainstorming, and the duck's own inspiration finally help it reach its new
home—with an entire community welcoming it with a parade!

Image Credits
Bao Phi author photo: Anna Min
p. 30 photos: Bao Phi

Designed by Kay Fraser

Printed and bound in China. PO3741

For everyone in my neighborhood, and everyone in yours —BP

"Hello! Happy May Day!" Hoa and Hue call to their neighbors.
Everyone is hurrying to the park for the May Day parade.
"Look!" says Hoa. She points to a colorful duck they've never
seen in the park before.

"Chao em!" Hue says.

"Hello, little duck!" Hoa says.

The duck totters back and forth. It seems confused.

"Are you lost?" Hoa asks the duck.

"QUACK!" the duck replies. It ruffles its feathers and kicks its webbed feet.

Hoa and Hue's friend Willow walks up and sees the duck. "Haŋ mitákuyepi!" Willow greets her friends. "Haŋ mitákuyepi!" she greets the duck.

"This duck seems lost," Hoa says to Willow. "Maybe we should help it get down to the pond."

"How do we do that?" Willow asks.

"Maybe with some food?" Hue suggests. "It might be hungry."
"Let's get a churro from Luis!" Willow says.

The three of them walk down the hill to where Luis helps his family sell churros and mangoes on a stick.

"Hi, Luis! Will you please help us?" Hue asks. "We saw a lost duck!"

Hue, Hoa, and Willow lead Luis back to the duck.

"It's a mandarin duck!" Luis says. He spends a lot of time watching ducks in the park, but he hasn't seen a mandarin here before.

"Bienvenido!" Luis says to the duck.

Hoa holds out a churro. The duck quacks and shakes its tail. It doesn't seem interested in churros.

"We probably shouldn't feed it anyway," Luis says. "I have to get back to the truck. Good luck, duck!"

Samatar rides up on his bike and skids to a stop. He's on his way to join the parade. "Soo dhawoow!" he says to the duck.
"We're trying to show this lost duck how to get to the pond," Hoa says.

Samatar squats down on his haunches and waddles like a duck. "Quack! Quack!" he says. "Follow me to your new home, friend."

But the duck just preens its feathers.

Sophea comes along on her skateboard. The wheels go *click clack click clack* over the cracks in the sidewalk. She kicks her skateboard up onto its back wheels to stop.

"Suasdey!" Sophea greets the duck.

"Can you help us get this lost duck to the pond?" Hoa asks.

Sophea nudges her skateboard toward the duck. "Hop on, duck! I'll give you a ride!"

"Quack!" The rolling skateboard startles the duck. It flaps its wings and skitters away down the sidewalk.

"You're heading toward the parade!" Sophea calls out.

Soon the friends find themselves in the middle of a crowd.
"Watch out, duck!"
They try to shoo the duck out of the way as a giant machine
made of bikes and drums slowly rolls by.

The duck hops onto Hoa's shoe for safety.

Some neighborhood kids come by, playing instruments.
"Meet our new friend!" Hue calls to them.
"Hello!" Junauda waves to the duck.
"Nyob zoo!" Tou calls out.
"Boozhoo!" Obediah says.
"Privet!" Aleksei shouts.
"Vannakam!" Sarojini says.

The musicians march around the little duck.
The duck marches in a circle.

They watch some people dressed in colorful feathers dance
and play drums. The duck flaps its feathers too.
"I think the duck is dancing!" Sophea says.

"Careful, ducky!" Willow says, as an Aztec
dancer steps close.

Three kids bounce over on their pogo sticks, curious to see what's happening.
"A new duck! Shalom!" Miriam says.
"Salam!" Farah says.
"Hej!" Oskar says.

"Quack!" says the duck, hopping up and down too.

"We're trying to help it get to the pond," Samatar explains.

"This way to the pond, duck!" Miriam bounces that way on her pogo stick.

The duck looks toward the pond. But suddenly a siren stops them all in their tracks.

Red and blue lights flash, startling the kids and their new friend. The duck quacks, makes a hop-jump, and flaps quickly away. The kids follow.

The duck lands. The police car is gone. Everything is quiet.
Hundreds of eyes have fallen on them.
They are in the parade!

"This mandarin duck is new in our neighborhood!" Hoa announces.
The kids hear people from the crowd shouting.
What are they saying?

The duck straightens its neck, stands tall, and begins to march.

The friends follow the duck.

The parade follows the friends!

The duck leads the parade all the way down to the pond.

Everyone gathers at its edge. The duck quacks cheerfully and flutters into the calm water. The kids laugh and cheer as the happy duck paddles its feet around its new home.

"Welcome!"

AUTHOR'S NOTE

I arrived as a six-month-old baby in a large, poor refugee family to Minnesota—one of 50 states created on the traditional, ancestral, and contemporary lands of Indigenous people, specifically the Dakota and Ojibwe. Some people welcomed us. Some very much did not.

MAYDAY PARADE 2019

I remember walking around Powderhorn Park in Minneapolis and seeing a lone duck standing by a muddy puddle, far away from the pond. I remember thinking I could relate to that duck, awkward and wondering if it belonged. Wondering who would be kind, and who would be cruel.

The annual MayDay Parade and Festival is a big deal in our community. It's collaboratively produced by In the Heart of the Beast Puppet and Mask Theatre, the MayDay Council, and Free Black Dirt, representing the many communities who call South Minneapolis home. It's where people come together for a better and more just world. I think of how difficult it is in our current age, when families are being torn apart by cruel immigration and deportation laws, or labeled "illegal" and made out to be "bad" people. My mother's fears, and my daughter's fears, of being taken away from everything they've known, are very real.

I wrote this book with hope that there are more of us who are willing to stand up for what's right, willing to say welcome, and willing to say we all belong.

—Bao Phi

MAYDAY PARADE 2019

LANGUAGES IN DUCK'S NEIGHBORHOOD!

Chao em (chow em) means "Hello, little brother/sister" in Vietnamese

Haŋ mitákuyepi (hon me-TALK-oo-yay-pee) means "Hello" in Dakota

Bienvenido (byehn-beh-NEE-thoh) means "Welcome" in Spanish

Soo dhawoow (so duh-whoa) means "Welcome" in Somali

Suasdey (sua-sdei) means "Hello" in Cambodian

Nyob zoo (N'yall zong) means "Welcome" in Hmong

Boozhoo (boo-zhoo) means "Hello" in Anishinaabe

Privet (pree-VYET) means "Hello" in Russian

Vannakam (va-na-ka-m) means "Welcome" in Tamil

Shalom (sha-LOW-m) means "Peace" in Hebrew

Salam (suh-LAM) means "Peace" in Arabic

Hej (hey) means "Hello" in Swedish

Ni hao (nee how) means "Hello" in Mandarin Chinese

Sawasdi (sa-wah-DEE) means "Hello" in Thai

Sabaidee (SAH-bye-dee) means "Hello" in Lao

Xin chao (seen chow) means "Welcome" in Vietnamese

Anyounghaseyo (ahn-nyeong-hah-seh-yo) means "Hello" in Korean

Tu loe mu na (tu loe mu na) means "Welcome" in Karen

With thanks to our language and content consultants: Sarah Park Dahlen, Nimo Farah, Ni Thaw Gay, Isela Gomez, Kathryn Haddad, David Kaminsky, Mai Neng Moua, Marcie Rendon, Siwaraya Rochanahusdin, Vidhya Shanker, Sopheak Tek, Saymoukda Vongsay, and Diane Wilson.

ABOUT THE AUTHOR

BAO PHI

Bao Phi is an award-winning poet and children's book author. His stunning debut picture book with illustrator Thi Bui, *A Different Pond*, won a Caldecott Honor, a Charlotte Zolotow Award, an Asian/Pacific American Award for Literature, an Ezra Jack Keats Honor, a Boston Globe-Horn Book Honor, and numerous other awards and accolades. *Hello, Mandarin Duck!* is his third children's book. Bao is a single co-parent father, an arts administrator, and a book nerd.

ABOUT THE ILLUSTRATOR

DION MBD

Dion MBD is an abbreviation for Dion's full name, which does not even fit on the first page of his passport. He is an Indonesian illustrator and designer who lives and works between Brooklyn, New York, and Bandung, Indonesia. He studied illustration at Ringling College in Florida, where he developed his fascination with clouds. In his downtime, Dion is either cooking, listening to John Mayer, or cloud watching.